Oi CAT!

Hodder
Children's
Books

Written by
Kes Gray

Illustrated by
Jim Field

"Oi CAT!

Step away from the gnat!"
said the frog.

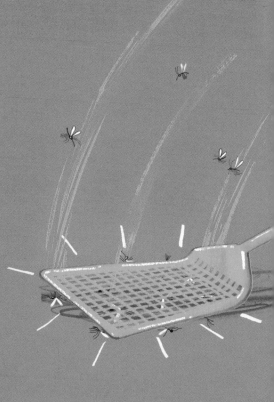

"But I hate gnats," said the cat. "Gnats are all **gnasty** and **gnibbly** and they keep biting me on the bottom!"

"That's right," smiled the frog, "I've changed the rules.

Dogs used to sit on **frogs,** but now they sit on **logs.**

And **cats** used to sit on **mats,** but now they sit on **gnats!"**

"It's a shame
you're not a **pony**,"
said the dog.
"If you were a pony
you could sit on some
macaroni."

"Just my luck,"
sighed the cat.

"If you were a **chick** you could sit on a **brick**," smiled the frog.

"If you were a **vole** you could sit on a **bowl**.

If you were a **leech** you could sit on a **peach**.

If you were a **duck** you could sit on a **truck!**"

"Well, I'm not a chick, am I?" frowned the cat.
"Or a vole, or a leech, or a duck."

"You're a **cat**,"
said the dog.

"On a **gnat**,"
smiled the frog.

"And rules are rules."

"If you were an **alpaca** you could sit on a **cream cracker,**" said the dog.

"If you were a **mink** you could sit on a **sink.**

If you were an **armadillo** you could sit on a **pillow,** a lovely soft comfy pillow."

"If you were a **lark** you could sit on a **shark,**" said the frog.

"Unbelievable," said the cat.

"If you were a **shrimp** you could sit on a **chimp**," said the dog.

"If you were a **bunny** you could sit on some **honey**.

If you were a **pheasant** you could sit on a **present**.

If you were a **troll** you could sit on a **doll!**"

"Whatever he sits on, it has to rhyme with cat," said the frog.

"Perhaps you could sit on a **bat!**" said the dog. "Instead of a mat or a gnat, you could sit on a cricket bat, or a baseball bat, or a softball bat!"

"Bats sit on **bats,"** said the frog.

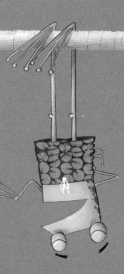

"What if you were a kitty instead of a cat?" said the dog.

"If you were a **kitty** you could sit on something **pretty** – like a pretty flamingo or some sparkly bows or some lovely colourful streamers!"

"**Dingoes** sit on **flamingos**,

crows sit on **bows**,

and **lemurs** sit on **streamers**," said the frog.

"How about a **mog**?" said the dog.
"If you were a **mog** you could sit on a **clog**. Or a **cog!**"

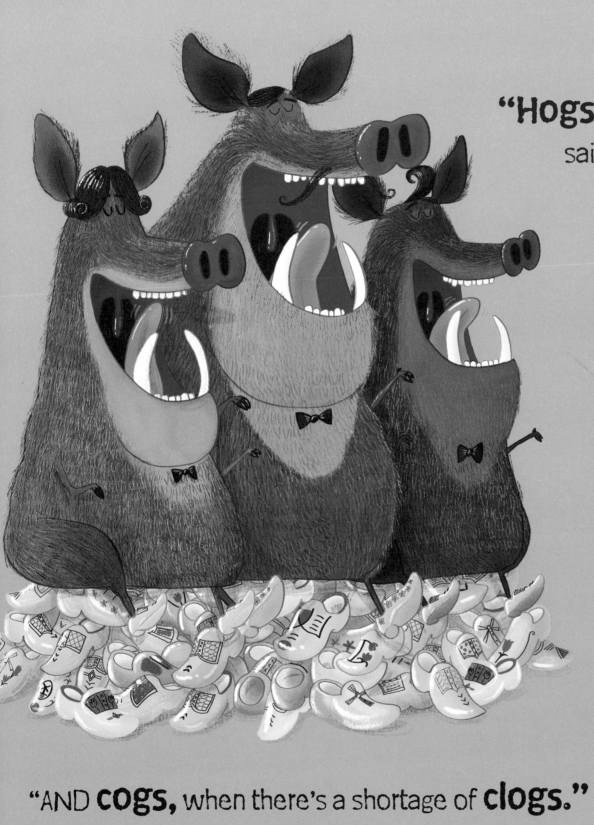

"Hogs sit on **clogs,"**
said the frog.

"AND cogs, when there's a shortage of **clogs."**

"Step away from the **frog!**"
frowned the frog.

"Yes, no one can sit on a
frog," nodded the dog.
"It has to be something that
rhymes with frog. Or mog
or clog or cog."

"Mmmm," said the cat, "what else rhymes with mog, frog, clog and cog? Let me think..."

GOG? JOG? BOG?
POG? ROG?
SOG? TOG?
UOG? VOG?
QUOG? ZOG?

DOG!

said the dog.
"Dog rhymes with
frog, mog, clog
AND COG!"

"So it does!" smiled the cat.

"So it does!"
clapped the frog.

"I wish I hadn't said that," said the dog.

LIFT ↑ FLAP

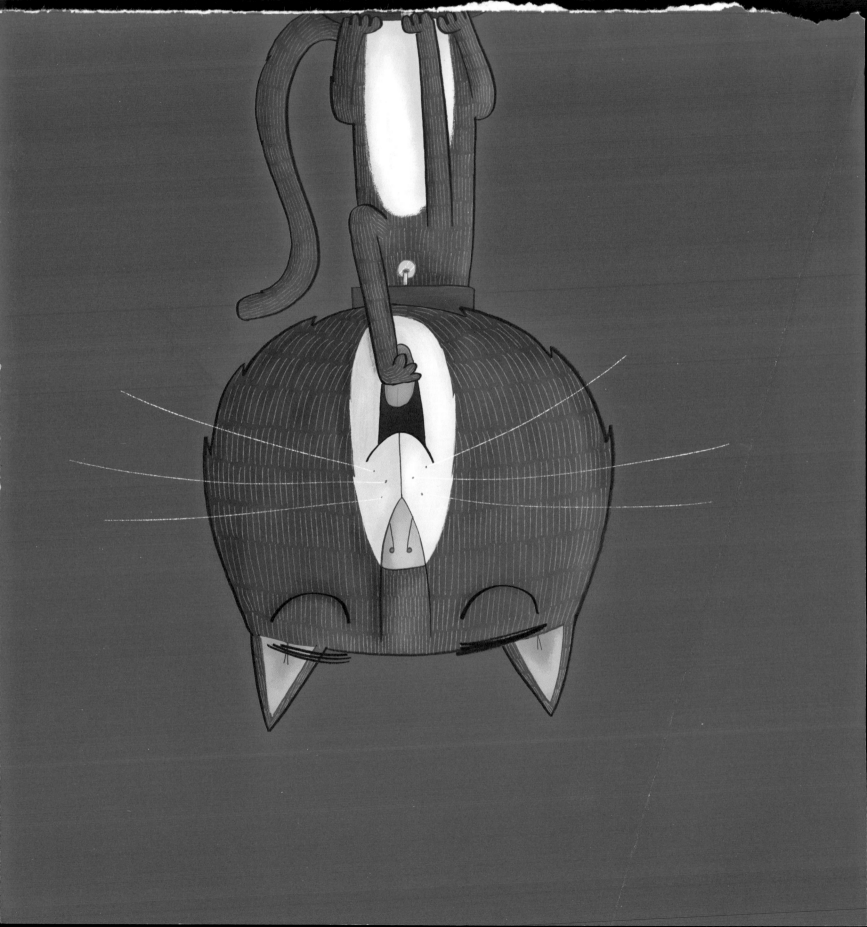